D1526295

THE JACK REACHER CASES (THE MAN WHO DIES HERE)

DAN AMES

SLOGAN BOOKS, NEW YORK NY

PRAISE FOR DAN AMES

"Fast-paced, engaging, original."

"Ames is a sensation among readers who love fast-paced thrillers."

"Cuts like a knife."

"Furiously paced. Great action."

FREE BOOKS AND MORE

**Would you like a FREE copy
of my story BULLET RIVER and the chance
to win a free Kindle?**

**Then sign up for the DAN AMES BOOK
CLUB:**

For special offers and new releases, sign
up here

THE MAN WHO DIES HERE

by

Dan Ames

1

There was no need to kill her quietly.

The market was a frenzy. People shouting. Cars and vans and buses groaning by with engines devoid of mufflers, coughing and spewing and sputtering. Live animals added to the cacophony. Monkeys, chickens, mules and several camels which were far from unusual in Marrakesh. It was the largest market in Morocco and it was a never-ending explosion of color, energy, noise and greed.

No one would much notice a dead woman, not until it was well too late, and as far as eyewitnesses and such, well, good luck to the authorities on that one.

The assassin's code name was Faust. He neither knew, nor cared, how and why he was called that. It had nothing to do with his real name, or his upbringing on a small farm in Holland. He supposed some genius at one of the many intelligence firms that employed him was bemused by the moniker, but again, he didn't care. As long as the money was deposited into the correct account, they could call him Sally and he wouldn't give it two thoughts.

Faust moved toward a stand selling spices. There were woven baskets full of the stuff. As impressive as their scents were, even more eye-catching were their colors: blazing orange, deep blues and reds, yellows, and greens. If you couldn't find the spice here, it didn't exist.

The girl did a very nice job of blending in, Faust noted. Morocco was still a primarily Muslim country, and she had gone with the modified hijab which covered most, but not all, of her face. It wasn't body length which revealed her black pants and black running shoes. It was enough of a disguise to pass at first glance, but upon closer inspection, an observer would accurately guess that she was not Moroccan but rather, European of some sort or possibly American or Canadian.

She was tall as well. Probably not six feet, but only two inches or so below it. She had broad shoulders and an overall look of fairly obvious athleticism.

Faust didn't know why she was being killed or who she was, other than a file and photo on paper.

That file was somewhat redacted, with original files featuring a fairly large amount of black ink crossing out key points that someone had deemed irrelevant for Faust, and possibly, others.

He watched as the woman moved confidently down the aisle of the market. She exhibited no curiosity; she had clearly been here many times before, knew what to expect, how to haggle, and was nonplussed by the pressure tactics of some of the street vendors.

Faust also noted that she must have spoken the language—there were no unnecessary hand gestures, confused expressions or elaborate pantomime.

Faust also noted the firm rebukes given to the most assertive of the salespeople. This woman was not afraid; she was comfortable and at ease.

All of which would make his job that much easier.

Faust had the obligatory white garb of the local men which fell to just below his knees. He wore dark brown boots instead of sandals, and to the interested observer, he too would probably not pass as a true native.

It didn't matter. No one was going to bother him. He was well over six feet, powerfully built, and moved with a purpose. He also had unusually colored eyes—so light brown they were almost golden in certain shades of the sun. His nickname growing up had been Wolf, and the art of intimidation had come early to him. His physical presence and the menace he could convey through his golden, glowing eyes gave most people pause.

The people at the Marrakesh market were no exception.

Beneath his robe Faust carried three

important items: a 9mm semi-automatic pistol, a silencer which was already screwed into place, and a dagger. The blade of the knife was honed to the absolute finest edge possible. Faust knew it would cut through the neck muscle, throat, and esophagus with incredible ease.

He hadn't planned how exactly he would kill her, whether it was gun knife or his bare hands. Faust would let the natural act of the woman's murder come about organically, and he would then utilize the right weapon at the right moment. It was his preferred technique and he found it always went more smoothly than forcing the moment to fit his pre-planned strategy.

Now, he moved forward, with extra energy behind his movement.

His golden eyes blazed as he moved in for the kill.

2

She knew they would come for her.

Eventually.

Two things surprised her: that they would choose here of all places and that they had spent some good money to try to take her out once and for all.

The guy was a professional, through and through. He didn't follow her obviously. He hung back, used reflections in windows and car windshields. He had the traditional garb of a local but with a decidedly upscale touch. There were dozens of men like him in the market, but she had spotted him almost instantly because she had been trained and her skills had been honed for many years.

The fact that they'd finally come for her didn't matter.

What mattered was they would fail.

And fail miserably.

It was really nothing for her to pretend as if everything was okay; she'd been doing that for far too long. Appear natural. Blend in. Show nothing. Give them nothing.

So she continued what she was doing which was getting some fresh air, looking for something to catch her eye but with no real goal of purchasing anything. It was a routine for her although she varied the time and location just to be safe.

Apparently, she hadn't varied it enough because they had found her.

And now, it seemed pretty clear they were going to try to kill her. The busy marketplace a perfect location for a murder. She had come to enjoy the market, its chaos, its social dynamics, humor, and color and life. That was it really. She came here to feel alive. Which was funny because now she was less than one hundred yards from someone who wanted to create the opposite result.

Well, she would have something to say about that.

3

Faust's wish came true.

He'd been following the woman, hoping she would turn into one of the many blind alleyways, out of the center of the throngs where he could dispatch her quietly and without too much alarm.

Oh, he wasn't fooling himself any: he knew a murdered white woman in the Marrakesh market would cause a stir. All he really needed was a little privacy to get the job done and perhaps five or ten seconds for him to be on his way before anyone thought to look for a killer.

And just like that, she granted him his wish.

At the end of the line of stands selling mostly meat: chicken, goat and beef - she seemed to disappear. He knew the market well enough, had scouted it on his dry runs after knowing her pattern of going to the market every few days. He also knew the alley beyond this section was a dead end filled with only a few vendors selling less desirable items: wicker baskets, awful jewelry, and cheap tourist watches made in Japan.

Faust moved quickly but appeared unhurried. He screwed the silencer onto the end of the pistol and thought how convenient the robe was to conceal an assassin's intentions.

"Buy one get one free," a vendor yelled at him in broken English. Faust almost smiled. Tried and true retail tactics were global, apparently.

He moved past the last vendor and turned into the alley.

His eyes tracked her most likely path, down to the left side of the narrow corridor where a few vendors were hawking wicker baskets.

But she wasn't there.

She was to the right, facing him.

And she was holding a basket in front of her, but the bottom had a hole in it and he could see that she had put her hand through it and in that hand was a gun.

In that moment Faust had an instantaneous flash of insight thinking about his name. Faust was a character associated with a lack of morals combined with ambition who ultimately pays the price for his sins.

It went through his mind in a brief second as he realized he had not steered her into the alley, rather, she had lured him to this spot.

The hunter had become the hunted.

He tried to raise his pistol, but even he knew it was a losing proposition: an assassin cocky with confidence, too slow and eager for blood to recognize the path of his own destruction.

Everything else he had planned was correct.

As the bullet crashed into his forehead,

followed by another just above his left eye, as his brains splashed out of the two brand-new holes in the back of his skull, it was as he had predicted: nothing happened in the alley for nearly ten seconds.

The man in the robe who sagged to the ground went unnoticed initially, long enough certainly for the woman to quietly exit the alley.

And then the body was discovered with its head missing most of the back of the skull.

People shouted. A woman screamed. But it wasn't quite as big a ruckus as Faust had predicted.

For the people selling the baskets, there was no profit in his death.

Faust would have laughed at the irony.

4

The letter was delivered by courier.
Lauren Pauling studied the envelope. Thick, creamy paper. Almost luxurious.

She studied the sender's return label. It, too, was elegant, printed in cursive with a gold foil backing, and it bore the name of one of New York's oldest and most prestigious law firms.

Since Lauren Pauling had retired from the FBI, she'd started her own security firm and sold it. That process had involved a fair amount of attorneys and legalese—so much so that Pauling had been very glad to be done with lawyers and their seemingly never-ending legal machinations.

It was probably cliché, but she felt a tiny amount of foreboding. In today's world, an unexpected letter from an attorney's office usually was bad news. Maybe a summons. Or a lawsuit. Or any number of possibilities, most of them bad.

Pauling opened the letter and scanned its contents. Apparently, she had been named in an estate settlement and her presence was requested at the law firm from which the letter originated. There was a date and a time and a statement that she would receive more information then.

Pauling frowned. Her parents were both deceased, and the only living relative was her sister, who lived in Oregon. She picked up her phone and sent her sister a text, asking if she too had gotten a letter about an estate settlement.

Her sister, always quick with a joke said, "No, but how can I get one?"

Pauling smiled.

But the frown returned.

Was it a scam? She double-checked the

law firms' name: Martin, David & Drexel. No, it couldn't be a scam—she knew the firm well. The letter was real; no typos, or cheap paper or any other signs of fraud.

Pauling circled the date on the calendar —it was only two days away—and had to admit her curiosity was aroused.

However, as so often happens in life, she put it in the back of her mind and two days later, arrived at the law offices of Martin, David & Drexel at the appointed time.

Waiting in the lobby, she saw her reflection. She was a mature woman with a slender build and a pretty face – or so she had been told. People also often mentioned they sensed in her an air of quiet confidence.

And her voice, of course, always received attention from men. They said she sounded like a whiskey-loving jazz singer.

Her lean face was tan—she'd just spent two weeks out west with Michael Tallon, her significant other, and they'd spent long days running in the desert near Death Valley. She'd never been in better physical condition, and her clothes fit her like never before.

The door whisked open and a man in a

silvery gray suit approached her. He was older, probably near sixty, with elegant eyeglass frames and a vintage Rolex.

"Ms. Pauling?" he asked.

"Yes."

"I'm John Martin. Please join me in our conference room—can my assistant get you anything? Coffee? Water?"

"No thank you," she replied.

The assistant, a smartly dressed young woman in a form fitting black business suit, held the door open for her. When it shut behind her, the silence was rich; it was the kind of law firm that prided itself on privacy and that was readily apparent.

The walls were painted a subtle ivory, the carpet an elegant gray. The doors were solid mahogany and the air reminded Pauling of a five-star hotel.

She followed Martin into a conference room where she was surprised to see a simple folder on a table with six empty chairs. The door to the conference room shut behind her, and Pauling looked at Martin.

"I'm confused," she said. "I thought this was an estate settlement. Not only do I not know whose estate we're about to discuss, but are you telling me I'm the only one named?"

"Please, let me explain," he said and gestured to a chair directly across from the folder. He took the chair opposite her. "I must apologize for the rather unusual circumstances but let me tell you why you're here."

Pauling waited for him to continue. His assistant appeared at the door with an espresso cup and handed it to Martin who thanked her and took a sip.

"Recently I was contacted by our partner firm in Paris," he said. "It seemed that one of their oldest and most valued clients had left a somewhat unusual request."

Pauling was even more confused. She had never had family in Paris, as far back as she could remember. In fact, she was pretty sure she didn't even know a single person in the City of Lights.

"It seems that this client had asked the firm to accomplish a certain task, which they failed to do," Martin continued. "In the event they had no other options, the client had left instructions to deliver this to you. I was asked to facilitate this initial meeting should you have any questions."

"I'm sorry—you're talking about this client in the past tense. Is he dead?"

"She is deceased, yes."

Now Pauling was even more intrigued. Her eyes found the folder in front of her.

"So this is *not* an estate settlement?" Pauling asks.

"Yes and no, as far as I know," he said. "They'll be able to answer that question for you in Paris."

Martin reached across and flipped open the folder. Inside was a short letter requesting Pauling's presence at yet another law firm—this one in Paris, along with a first-class airline ticket and an envelope.

"There is enough cash in there to cover any expenses," the attorney said. "A very nice hotel has also been booked for you."

Pauling was losing her patience. She had no intention of flying to Paris with such little information. "I'm not going anywhere until I know who this mystery client is and why she wants me included in whatever is going on here," she said. Pauling swiveled slightly in her chair, her body language indicating she was ready to get up and leave if he wasn't more forthcoming.

Martin reached out and tapped the bottom of the letter, which showed a name: Josephine Moutier.

Pauling had seen it and registered no memory of anyone with that name. "I don't know any Moutier," she said.

"I believe that is her maiden name," Martin said. "She reverted back to it toward the end of her life."

"What was her married name?"

Martin looked at her. "Reacher," he said.

5

ZURICH

IT WAS a rare thing to die twice.

She supposed it had happened before. Certainly, over the years and decades and centuries, it was possible. Likely even. A soldier on the battlefield pronounced dead only to survive, and then later eventually die of natural causes. That could be considered dying twice.

Her situation was a little bit different.

She had died first as a woman named

Gunnella Bohm. Head of one of the world's largest crime syndicates known as the Zurich Collective. An Italian businessman had exacted revenge and used a shotgun to blow her off the deck of his yacht.

But she had survived, even though the world had announced her death.

She, too, had allowed Gunnella Bohm to die.

Instead, she had been reborn as Goda Becher. Head of a rival syndicate known as Zeta. That syndicate's end hadn't been as flashy; simply a foiled plot to make the mega wealthy individuals even richer.

So, she herself had killed "Goda Becher" but saved the initials, just not the identity.

Which was better, because now she was going to back to being Gunnella Bohm, in all her glory.

She stood now, naked in front of the bathroom mirror in her high rise in Zurich. She had several residences scattered throughout the world, all under assumed names and identities with bills paid automatically by a fat savings account, also in Zurich.

She was a big woman, well over six feet.

Solid, with broad shoulders, wide hips and big feet and hands. In some ways, her face was more noble than beautiful.

Bohm rarely went out of the apartment. Everything was delivered, food, medicine, booze, and human flesh. The pretty young thing on the bed right now was worn out. Bohm had been very rough on her, and she would have to pay her a bonus to keep her delicious mouth shut.

The anger was always there, but this time it had come from bad news. Her assassin in Marrakesh had failed miserably to kill the young woman who'd been his target. Instead, she had killed him. Which was just as well because Gunnella Bohm would have had him killed anyway. Failure was not an acceptable outcome.

As she often did, a habit drilled into her by her overbearing father, Gunnella did not overreact. Instead, she contemplated her options. Life was a chessboard, and the techniques used in the game: attack, retreat, feint, capture and her favorite, forking (when an opponent had to choose which piece to sacrifice thanks to a strategically placed knight), were always the best strategies.

So, the girl had escaped in Morocco.

Just another moving piece on the board.

Bohm walked to the balcony, slid open the glass doors and stepped out onto her balcony. It was cold, and she felt her nipples harden. Her balcony was private, and she was high up in the lone penthouse apartment, naturally—so causing a scene was not something she was worried about. It was a bit of compensation for not being able to go out as often as she might like and often having to wear disguises.

The ultimate freedom was being naked with fresh, biting cold air against her skin and nothing but sky and the city before her.

Bohm felt her vigor return and with it, her sex drive.

She breathed deeply for five minutes, then returned to the apartment and withdrew a leather whip. It was short, with a braided tip.

The girl was going to be hurting badly when she was done with her.

Bohm knew whatever bonus she was going to give the poor thing wasn't going to be nearly enough.

6

"Champagne?"

The flight attendant smiled down at Pauling. He was a slender black man with a pronounced forehead and a single hoop in his left ear.

"I believe I will," Pauling said. "Thank you." She accepted the glass and set it on her tray table. She was indeed in first class, as the attorney back in New York had said, and was on the way to Paris.

She glanced out the window. They were well above any clouds and the last remaining light was fading fast. Soon, it would be dark, and the champagne might help ease her into a contented slumber. She never had much trouble with jet lag, and if she was fatigued upon her arrival, the good law firm in Paris, and their client, had been considerate enough to give her time at the hotel to recover from the flight before the appointment.

Pauling had seen quite a bit of life in her years on Earth. During her years in the FBI, she'd covered everything from murder, drugs and counterfeiting to arson, rape, and serial killers.

Few things surprised her anymore.

Except Jack Reacher.

When he had come into her life, back on a case that had collided with her last investigation with the FBI, it had been a whirlwind of unexpected occurrences. The case itself had taken them overseas and ended with an epic battle with seasoned and deadly mercenaries.

And then Reacher had left. Just walked right out of her life, as of yet, never to appear again.

He had been honest with her; he was not interested in settling down. He had an ATM card, a toothbrush and the clothes on his back, not much else.

Still, the ramifications of her brief relationship had created a surprising number of echoes.

Like this one.

She had been named as a party in the estate settlement of a woman whose married name had been Reacher.

Pauling supposed it was theoretically possible Jack Reacher had gotten married, and Josephine Moutier Reacher was his wife, but she didn't think so.

For one thing, but it would be odd for there to be an estate issue as she would most likely have been fairly young, most likely Pauling's age or younger. Of course, it wasn't unheard of for a woman to die in her forties or fifties. Cancer, cardiac disease, car accidents.

Still, it was unlikely.

The more realistic scenario was the woman had been Reacher's mother. She certainly would have been old, probably in her eighties at least.

Pauling remembered vaguely him saying

something about his mother and possibly mentioning Paris. So that would be the obvious answer.

Unfortunately, Pauling knew precious little of Reacher's family. His brother Joe had worked in Treasury. Had Joe been married? Kids? Pauling knew he had died in the line of duty—a counterfeiting case in Georgia, if she remembered correctly.

Pauling sipped her champagne.

Jack Reacher was so different from Michael Tallon, but in some ways very similar. They were two of the strongest men she'd ever known. They each had a similar quality that said *I'm not looking for a fight, but if you start it, I'll finish it.*

The difference was stability, in a lot of ways. Tallon was stable: he had a ranch near Death Valley, a cell phone, and a desire for a steady relationship. All of those were the complete opposite of Jack Reacher.

Pauling had grown to feel a connection with Michael Tallon she'd never felt with any other man, including Reacher.

But Reacher somehow had a way of reappearing in her life, if not physically.

She eventually drifted off and was awakened by the announcement they had arrived at their destination. Pauling disembarked, found the driver and car the law firm had arranged to meet her, and was soon whisked to an upscale hotel in the heart of Paris. She checked into her room and was pleased to see a welcome basket with bottled water and fresh fruit. A pot of coffee soon arrived as well.

She wasn't tired, so she decided to unpack her few belongings and go for a walk.

Pauling loved Paris and had been there several times both on business and for pleasure. Now, it was cold and rainy, but she savored the fresh air and the element of the unknown. She walked for nearly an hour taking in the sights and sounds of one of the greatest cities in the world. Pauling stopped in at her favorite bookstore in the world: Shakespeare and Company, an old haunt of Ernest Hemingway's.

Eventually, Pauling made her way back to the hotel and took a short nap. When she awakened, it was time to get ready for the meeting. She dressed conservatively and another car and driver took her to the firm. It was located in a building three hundred years old and was the European equivalent of the law office she'd just been in New York.

The process was nearly identical: she waited in an exquisitely adorned lobby and was then whisked away to a conference room after being offered coffee and water by an assistant.

Soon, a woman entered, about Pauling's age. She had blonde hair neatly brushed back and a power business suit. It either had padded shoulders or the woman was born with an impressive upper body.

"Hello, Ms. Pauling," the woman said "My name is Amanda Brody. I represent the estate of Josephine Moutier Reacher."

Pauling nodded.

"First, a few forms for you to look over," Brody said.

Pauling scanned the documents. She had no intention of signing anything. She was really here out of curiosity.

However, the first page was simply a confidentiality agreement, saying Pauling wouldn't discuss the terms of the meeting with anyone else.

Pauling set the confidentiality agreement aside. She wouldn't sign until she learned more.

Brody didn't seem fazed by her reluctance. She proceeded.

"Our client has left a codicil in her will. It's somewhat simple. In the event certain individuals were unable to accomplish certain tasks, we were to contact you and reach an arrangement."

"An arrangement for what?" Pauling asked.

Brody's eyes glanced at the confidentiality agreement.

"Look, I don't have any intention of signing any document until I know what this is about," Pauling said. "*If* it appears legitimate, and it's something within the realm of possibility, I'll sign the confidentiality agreement. But I'm not doing it the other way around."

Brody exhaled and reached for a folder.

It appeared to Pauling that law firms the world over used the same envelope supplier:

it was nearly identical to the one in New York.

Brody flipped it open.

"Ms. Reacher has instructed us to reach an agreement with you. In exchange for your help, we will pay you a sum that is negotiable but will be no less than two million dollars."

Pauling was surprised yet again, although she didn't show it. She'd been at enough negotiation tables to have an inscrutable poker face.

"What is the assignment?" Pauling asked.

Brody withdrew an 8 x 10 photo of a woman. She had blue eyes, sandy hair, and a classically beautiful face. But there was something off in her expression, as if she'd seen something that had given her pause. A haunted expression if Pauling had ever seen one.

"To find this woman."

Pauling thought none of it made sense. For starters, two million dollars was ridiculous for a simple missing person's case. Yet, that wasn't all that didn't make sense. If the woman was indeed Jack Reacher's mother, did that mean the missing woman was a relative of Reacher's too? A sister? And if so, why hadn't Reacher's mother asked her son to find her? Jack Reacher was the best investigator Pauling had ever seen. Hands down.

"If you'll excuse my direct approach," Pauling asked. "Why would your client pay me two million dollars for a simple missing person's case? Why not just go to the police?"

"Because we're not the only ones looking for her. Time is of the essence."

"I don't understand."

"The other people looking for her don't just want to find her."

Brody looked directly into Pauling's eyes.

"They want to kill her."

7

"Who wants to kill her?" Pauling asked.

"Unfortunately, that we don't know." Brody said. "Since certain associates hired by our client have been unable to even locate her, we're not entirely certain who the bad actors are."

"Have they tried to kill her? As in actual attempted murder?"

"We believe so. However, without being able to find her, we can't know for certain."

"I see," Pauling said.

She began to ask another question, but Brody held up her hand.

"Everything you need is in that folder,"

she said. "Why don't you take it with you, study its contents, and contact me if you have any further questions?"

"Our client has provided an operating fund for you." Brody slid an ATM card and a credit card to Pauling. "Virtually unlimited, within reason."

"What about an associate?" Pauling asked. "If I bring someone onto my team, I'm assuming the confidentiality agreement doesn't apply."

"It still applies, but you are then held responsible for any breaches from your team," Brody said.

Pauling smiled. Brody was definitely a skilled attorney.

Pauling pocketed the two cards and scooped up the folder.

"I'm sure I'll be in touch," Pauling said. She left the law firm and went to a cafe where she bought an espresso, carrying it back to her hotel room. Her room had a desk and chair so she sat down with the coffee, sipped, and opened the folder.

The first document was pretty simple: it

contained the photo of the woman, along with a brief biographical sketch.

Pauling studied the photo, first. The woman was young in the photo, a teenager most likely. She had a smooth face, strong jaw, and considerable cheekbones. Her nose was narrow and her eyes were blue.

A good-looking young woman, but not a dazzling beauty that would stop a person in his or her tracks. Somewhere between above average yet also, someone who would blend in anywhere and go relatively unnoticed. No distinguishing features, nothing out of the ordinary. In the photo, she had on a wool sweater, and her face looked slightly flushed.

Pauling read the information below the photo.

Noelle Sinclair.

Parents unknown.

Last place of residence: Paris, France.

No fingerprints on file.

No known relatives.

Last known address: 22 Rue des Lilacs.

Pauling frowned. It was so odd: why didn't the girl have either Reacher's name or his mother's maiden name? Where did

Sinclair come from? How was she related and if she wasn't, why was the term estate case being thrown around?

Pauling was disappointed there was no mention of the girl's education. That would have ordinarily been included and been a treasure trove of information: addresses on file, photos, known friends and associates.

How long had the girl been out of touch with her family members that they had so few details of her life? Or did they have them and just don't want to share?

Pauling set the page aside and went back to the folder.

But it was empty.

That was it.

She got up from the desk and went to the bed, stretched out on it, and put her hands behind her head.

The ceiling was immaculate, with crown molding dusted in some sort of gold filigree. Nice hotel. Too bad she was here alone.

That was the beauty of being a single woman, unattached, in the stricter sense.

She could leave and go home. Call up the attorney and say no thanks. She didn't have time to be running around looking for some missing woman who was possibly being chased by a mysterious boogeyman.

On the other hand, Paris was beautiful this time of year. She had an unlimited operating fund and a potential payout of a cool two million dollars. Nothing to sneeze at.

None of that really mattered though.

She'd always said once she sold her firm that she would only take cases that held a special interest for her. Something that either intrigued her or was for a good cause.

This might be both.

It certainly intrigued her: a missing young woman who may or may not be a relative of Jack Reacher. Someone potentially alone with a price on her head.

Even if it was a prank or a wild goose chase, Pauling was willing to give it a day or two. Some initial investigation and then she would be back in the States in no time.

Still, she was no fool. She was alone in a big city, about to undergo at least a preliminary investigation that may or may not involve more than one murder attempt.

Pauling had no weapon.

Which is why she had asked about bringing on an associate.

Pauling smiled at the ceiling.

A question had popped into her mind.

What the hell was Michael Tallon doing right now?

8

Tallon's hands were covered in blood. He slid the knife in and continued to work around the mule deer's bones. It was a standard size buck, and he'd taken it with a single shot from nearly four hundred yards out.

Now, he was skinning the animal a good distance from his home. No need to attract scavengers.

It took him nearly three hours to properly harvest the deer's meat. He would pack it into his freezer and enjoy it for a good long time. Tonight, however, he would have venison steaks with a couple of ice-cold beers.

His small ranch was located within a stone's throw from Death Valley, and he used the rugged terrain to stay in shape. He either hiked or ran nearly every day, rain or shine, blazing heat, or deadly blazing heat.

It didn't matter.

Tallon thought of his body as the edge of a knife: keep it sharp or let it get dull and useless.

Back at his ranch, he cleaned up and started a fire. He would grill the steaks old school: over an open flame.

He wished he wasn't going to be eating alone, again.

Tallon had hoped Lauren Pauling, his love interest, would be spending more time with him. She had certainly been to the ranch for extended stays but she always eventually went back to New York.

And now she had flown to Paris for some reason.

It was taking some getting used to: all of his life he had been the one unwilling to commit. He had been the cliché soldier: always off to the next battlefield, the girlfriend back home worrying about if he'd ever come back.

It had been part of the reason he had never settled down: his occupation didn't make it easy. So he had played the field for far too long.

He was older now and experienced in every sense of the word. When he'd met Pauling, he'd felt like he'd found a partner. Not only was she intelligent, beautiful, incredibly sexy, and a formidable person in general, she understood his business. Being a former FBI agent, she knew what it was like to try to have a relationship with someone whose job wasn't garden variety. It wasn't a 9 to 5 deal, just like hers hadn't been.

He went to the refrigerator and grabbed a bottle of beer, twisted off the cap and took it to the fire. He sat down, put his feet up and gazed out at the distant mountains. It was dusk and there was just the slightest fringe of red at the edges of the night sky. The stars would soon be out. He heard a coyote's bark and wondered if they'd picked up the scent of his deer.

So I'm not alone after all, he thought.

He went into the kitchen, where he'd put the venison steaks. He'd applied a rub of salt, pepper, onion powder, garlic powder and paprika. They would crust up nicely over the flames.

Tallon took the meat to the fire and placed it on a cast iron pan, coated with butter.

The meat sizzled and the smoke wafted up into the thin air. It smelled great. There were some leftover greens in the fridge he would pair with the venison, and then he would probably switch to red wine.

Later, maybe he'd watch a movie.

Perhaps a French film.

He smiled in the darkness.

Set in Paris.

9

Pauling had the hotel arrange for a car rental and the concierge called to tell her it was ready. She had a breakfast of eggs, bacon, fresh fruit and black coffee.

It was a Reacher kind of breakfast, except for the fresh fruit. The only time she remembered Reacher eating fruit was if it was stuffed into a pie crust.

Pauling smiled at the memory. Working on a Reacher-related case and now she was ordering food like him. She hoped she wouldn't start traveling with a toothbrush and an ATM card and wear the same clothes for weeks at a time.

She paid for her meal and returned to her room. Before she set out on a boots-on-the-ground investigation, she would get some other things in motion. She scanned and uploaded all of the documents she'd received in the attorney's office and sent them to her best cyber sleuth back in the U.S.

He had worked for her when she'd had her own firm and he was now a very successful freelancer. Pauling suspected that either he, or someone in his employ, had some hacking ability because he was often able to find information not available on any public servers.

With that done, she also sent the image of the woman to a friend still at the FBI. The Bureau had an excellent facial recognition database tied to Interpol. If the young woman's face was on file with any law enforcement organization in Europe, they would get a hit.

Satisfied that she'd set the wheels in motion on the digital front, she decided to begin the real-world investigation.

The car was an Audi sedan and she headed out toward the address in the file. It was on the western edge of the city, a low-to-middle class residential neighborhood.

The sky was overcast and the hint of rain was on the horizon. It was a busy morning, traffic wise, and Pauling drove carefully but confidently. She'd been to France many times before and was capable behind the wheel.

Pauling soon found herself on a narrow street with beige colored stone houses on either side of her, most of them behind iron gates adorned with flowers as if to soften the message of *keep out*.

Cars were parked along one side of the street, occasionally a van or delivery truck would be taking up too much room and she would have to wait for the other vehicle or, more likely, bicycle, to pass before she could proceed on her route.

The Audi was bigger than most cars here. She figured the hotel had assumed the American would want a big car. Well, she wasn't complaining. It was a nice vehicle.

Finally, Pauling came to the address and had to go two blocks north to park. She found a space for the Audi and then walked back to the location. So far, it was the only thing she really had to go on.

22 Rue de Lilacs had none of the flowers mentioned in the name. It was a single family home, plaster and stone, in relatively good condition. Two stories, with shutters recently painted green and a chimney that had a hairline crack visible from the street. There were fresh flowers on the doorstep and a dark red Opal in the driveway.

Pauling knocked on the door.

Moments later, a woman answered.

She had jet black hair pulled back over her shoulders and she had on shorts and a T-shirt as if she'd just gotten back from a walk or jog.

The woman said "Bon jour" and Pauling spoke in passable French and the woman said, "I speak English if you prefer."

Pauling smiled. There hadn't been a trace of accent in the woman's English.

Pauling held up the photo of Noelle Sinclair. "This girl is missing," she said. "Do you have any idea where she might be? This is her last known address."

"Sorry, I don't know her," the woman said.

She had only given the photo the briefest of glances.

"How long have you lived here?" Pauling asked.

The woman's eyes narrowed. "Why is that any of your concern?"

Pauling smiled. "It's not really *my* concern. The young woman has people who care about her and I'm just curious if you lived her at the same time as her, or perhaps after."

The woman's dark eyes flashed irritation and Pauling saw no reason why. Maybe she was having a bad day. Or maybe she was hiding something.

"We bought it six months ago. At auction. It was abandoned."

"Did the previous owners have any mail delivered here? With a name or a forwarding address."

"No. I have no idea who owned it or who lived here or who this girl is. Sorry."

It was a curt dismissal and Pauling decided not, for the moment, to pressure the woman. She could always come back and

play the bad cop, now that she'd demon-
strated the role of good cop.

"Thank you for your time," Pauling said.
The woman shut the door quickly and
Pauling walked back to the Audi. As she did,
she saw a man two houses down watching
her. She veered away from the car and
walked down the street toward the man.

As she did so, he abruptly turned and
went into his house, slamming the door shut.

Even from that distance, Pauling could
hear the interior lock rammed home.

She stopped and walked back to the Audi.

Who says the French aren't friendly? she
thought.

10

The cuffs of his tailored shirts were monogrammed. RKR: Ronald Richard Kingsley. CEO of Kingsley Holdings, former politician, intelligence officer and fixer for several European strongmen, frequently seen on television interviews giving his highly valued take on current affairs.

He caught his reflection in the window and was pleased as always: he was a man who became more handsome with each passing year. Salt and pepper hair with just the slightest bit of wave, strong jaw and aristocratic nose. His posture was always impeccable and he knew he was the kind of man who, upon entering a room, immediately became the center of attention. He was used to it, and unabashedly enjoyed it.

The ceiling in his office was a fresco two hundred years old, bordered in gold, featuring an angel, blue sky and clouds.

"Bertram to see you," his assistant said. She was in her early twenties, just out of university and she wore the tight black dress he insisted all of his assistants wear. Her body was shapely, taut and reminded him of a skillfully carved musical instrument – maybe a violin – that just needed an expert's hands and skill to be played correctly. Once plucked and stroked perfectly, it would make wonderful music.

It made him hard just thinking about it.

"Thank you Kerstin," he said.

He watched her leave and her narrow hips didn't sway – they seemed to pulsate with each step. She glanced back at him and he didn't avert his eyes.

Next week, he thought to himself. Next week he would invite her to dinner and bed her that same night. She was new, and he tended to wait just a bit before asserting himself. But he could tell she was ready.

As she left the office, an older man wearing a rumpled gray suit entered the office. Bertram Pohler was an attorney, administrator and chief of staff for Kingsley. Sometimes Kingsley thought of Pohler as his own personal dark cloud following him around, always trying to blot out the light.

"What now...?" Kingsley snapped.

He hated being interrupted – especially when he was having reveries about one of his new assistants. He realized the logic flaw; if there were no interruptions there would be no need for his spectacularly sexy assistant to visit him. Unless he created a pretense but that was beneath him.

Pohler shut the door.

So dramatic, Kingsley thought.

"It seems there have been some recent developments with Zurich," Pohler said.

Kingsley felt his back stiffen, and his face began to warm with anger.

"Goddamnit," he said.

"It seems there was an assassination attempt in Marrakesh."

"Since you said *attempt*," Kingsley said, "I'm correct in assuming it was a failure?"

"Yes. The would-be assassin was killed instead."

Kingsley shook his head. Over the years, he had marveled often at the resourcefulness of his quarry, but every new occurrence raised his grudging admiration even more. Recently, they'd been tipped off on the possible location of their target and that had taken their actions to a whole new level.

"So..."

"Steps are being taken for a new plan," Pohler said.

"Great," Kingsley responded, his voice bereft of enthusiasm.

"However, that's not all."

This time, Kingsley snapped. "Christ, man – get on with it!"

"It seems that an American has begun asking questions in Paris. Possibly even starting an investigation."

"An American? Why on Earth? Who?"

Pohler's face had gone gray. It looked like he had swallowed something poisonous and was about to spit it out. "Apparently she is a former FBI agent."

Kingsley slammed his hand down on his desk. The day had just gone from bad to much, much worse.

"Why in the hell would an American FBI agent–"

"Former."

"–be involved?"

"I'm still trying to figure that out. She visited a law firm and after that, began making inquiries."

"Well find out which law firm, what lawyer, and anything else you can. Put your best surveillance team on it – the whole shebang: on the street, electronic, digital. I want this woman's every move tracked and reported."

"Of course."

Pohler waited.

"What? Get going!" Kingsley bellowed.

The older man scurried from the room.

Kingsley sat down at his desk and drummed his fingers on its wooden surface.

His mind drifted back to his assistant and which restaurant he should choose to begin his conquest. The fact that she would make the reservation for them made it all the sweeter.

Kingsley pictured her in bed underneath him. He was angry, frustrated and eager to dish out some physical punishment. He would take out his fury on Kerstin.

He wondered with more than a little indifference, if she would like it.

11

P auling found an outdoor café, parked, and ordered a coffee. She dug out her laptop and connected to the café's Wi-Fi.

So far, there was no news on her digital inquiries, but she had an idea.

The woman at the address where Noelle Sinclair had last lived said they'd bought the house at auction. Auctions were public transactions, at least, Pauling reasoned, they were back in the United States. Why would it be any different in France?

She spent the better part of a half hour digging through Parisian real estate databases. Eventually, Pauling had success by using the property address as her main search tool. Soon, she found the information in the auction house's records.

22 Rue de Lilacs had sold for nearly two hundred thousand Euros. Pauling studied the list of names associated with the deal: real estate agents, bankers, insurance people, but found no mention of the owner. She wondered if that was on purpose: perhaps a policy against naming individuals in a public auction transaction?

Momentarily thwarted, Pauling scoured the information two more times before deciding the auction house had not included the seller's information. She studied the names of the real estate agents and other professionals involved in the sale. Of the agents listed, Pauling noted the last one, figuring he would be the lowest ranking of the three.

She found the phone number for the firm and asked for the agent. When he answered, Pauling identified herself as the current owner of 22 Rue de Lilacs and that she had discovered a small box of belongings that must be the property of the past seller. Was there a forwarding address where she could send the box? She hadn't opened the package, she said, but assumed it might be something valuable.

The man asked if it was okay to put her on hold. She said yes.

Pauling waited. After nearly two minutes, she was convinced the man was checking with his superiors to see if it was allowed to give out that information and they were probably in the process of telling him no, that was against the rules. And maybe they were even right now discussing how to find out her location because she was probably impersonating the owner.

A little paranoid, sure, but not out of the question. Pauling had learned in the FBI to always think of things as possible contingencies and avoid including emotion in the assessment.

Instead of her worst-case scenario, the man came back on the line and simply said to forward the box to a Charles Altamont of 1503 Rue de Vixom.

Pauling thanked him, hung up, and punched in the address on her phone's navigation app. It was an hour's drive north of Paris. She guzzled her coffee and fired off messages to the investigators looking into Noelle Sinclair. She told them to add a Charles Altamont to the search, along with the address she'd been given and inform her as soon as possible when they had something.

Pauling snapped her laptop closed and went back to the Audi.

A drive in the countryside north of Paris.

She could handle that.

12

It was a dry white wine, perfectly chilled. The setting sun gave it an almost metallic glow, shining through the crystal wineglass, the din of traffic far below. Gunnella Bohm's big hand cupped the wineglass and she brought it to her plump lips, sipped slowly, savored the rich bouquet with the subtlest hints of fruit.

The satellite phone on the glass-topped table next to her buzzed imperceptibly. She glanced at the screen. She knew the code by heart.

Bohm picked up the phone feeling ridiculous she had to use it. However, encryption was key and the technology on the device was state-of-the-art, impossible to intercept or record. She used it because her client in Paris demanded it. It was annoying, but he paid on time and he paid well.

"Yes," she said.

There was no need for an introduction. "You have failed me," Kingsley said. Bohm could picture him, in his ridiculous monogrammed shirt, probably in his fancy office with his assistant nearby, ready to pour him a whiskey or light a cigar, kowtow to him in any way possible. Bohm wasn't judging – it was the exact same level of obedience she demanded of her own staff.

"The job is not yet complete," Bohm said. "That does not constitute a failure, simply a slight delay."

"You have a solution in mind?"

"I do."

Bohm briefly described the new plan she had come up with. Kingsley grudgingly approved, but not without a warning.

"There will be no third strike. Fail this time, and you're out," he said. "Permanently."

She smiled inwardly. Bohm was afraid of no one. Certainly not Ronald Richard Kingsley. She'd dealt with men ten times more dangerous than him, and survived.

Barely, but she survived.

Bohm took another sip of wine and dialed a new number. Technically, Kingsley had been correct, of course. It had been a failure, and a bad one.

But Bohm had a solution. A somewhat unconventional choice, but she'd had her eye on this one for some time and thought this was the perfect time and opportunity to turn the asset loose.

13

The tall, elegant black woman known as "Star" saw the number on her cell phone on the passenger seat next to her. It had no name attached, but she knew who it was.

Star was an up-and-comer within an organization of contract killers loosely but appropriately called the Department of Murder.

A former aspiring actress from Los Angeles, Star fell into her profession thanks to a stunt woman she'd met on a job. That woman had helped train her for a martial arts movie, and in the process, shared a side hustle.

Killing people for money.

Like the guy in the trunk.

Star drove a black Cadillac and now, she exited the freeway and talked to a go-between who represented another shady organization known as the Zurich Collective.

More accurately, a woman named Gunnella Bohm.

Star listened and didn't hesitate. The number being offered had an extra zero compared to most of her jobs and that kind of money was something she had never even dreamed was possible.

Yes, she would take the job, and yes, she could start right away.

After agreeing to look at the details as soon as she was able, Star disconnected the call and drove straight out to the desert, past a closed road and down a flat valley she'd used before.

Hidden from view, she pulled the Cadillac over and popped the trunk.

The dead man was wrapped in a ten-thousand-dollar Persian carpet. It was a damn fine carpet and Star had considered keeping it, but there was simply too much blood.

The dead man was a Hollywood producer who'd scammed some Mob guys and thought he was too rich and powerful to be taken out.

He had figured wrong.

Star grabbed the ropes she'd used to roll up the producer's body and heaved it from the Cadillac. She dragged the parcel to the lip of a narrow crevice. It was merely twenty yards long but very deep and the opening was barely a foot wide. Just enough room to slide through a body.

The crevice was impossible to see from above and there was no way to get to the bottom – save bringing out some heavy duty earth moving vehicles and trench the whole thing wider and why would anyone want to do that? She always stripped her targets of any and all technology so unless someone had a GPS tracker on her or her car, there was no need to worry about discovery.

With the producer deeply immersed in his new role, Star got back in the Caddy and connected her phone's music player via Bluetooth.

Up on her playlist was the Rolling Stones.

Let It Bleed.

You bet I will, she thought.

14

The drive north from Paris was not what Pauling had expected. She'd pictured rolling hills full of flowers reminiscent of Monet's garden. What she experienced was bumper-to-bumper traffic, stop and go then stop again, with most of her time spent on the Audi's brake pedal instead of the accelerator.

When she was finally able to leave the main road, Pauling quickly found herself on a narrow one-way street, with a forested bluff on her left and a chest-high stone wall on her right. She had no idea what would happen if she met a car going the other way. Someone would have to back up and if it was her, she would have to go nearly a mile for a turnaround.

The landscape was strange to Pauling; it felt like part farmland, part castle ruins. There were occasional A-frame style homes that looked abandoned, along with centuries-old stone buildings without windows and a few had turrets.

The only way Pauling could tell for certain if the homes were inhabited was the occasional car or van parked in the pebbled driveway. She had yet to see an actual living person.

When she saw a vehicle, she was struck by how anachronistic it looked: this area had virtually no newer construction, instead everything had been made with a taupe colored stone and dark timbers.

It was charming in a way, but she also wondered about the economics of the place. How many were abandoned? And why?

Eventually, she made her way to the address her search had produced: 1503 Rue de Vixom. It was a two-story stone house with beige shutters and a faded red clay tile roof. There was a gold-colored four-door sedan parked in front.

Pauling pulled the Audi next to it, parked, and walked to the front door. The driveway was crushed stone and a recent rain had turned the ground beneath it to mud.

She looked for a doorbell or knocker of some kind but saw none. She wrapped her knuckles on the wood door. It was painted white, and the paint was peeling along the edges. She could smell wood smoke maybe from a fireplace – it was gray and overcast, the smell of rain was in the air, too. Maybe someone was planning for the storm that was sure to come.

The door opened and an older man peered out at her. He had gray hair, a silver bushy beard and was dressed in dark corduroy pants and a heavy sweater. A pipe was in his mouth.

"American?" he asked, in English, a smirk hiding beneath his beard and moustache.

"Yes," Pauling answered. "Are you Charles Altamont?"

A gust of wind pushed against the house

and a smattering of heavy raindrops began to fall.

"Why don't you come in before the clouds deliver their bounty?"

Pauling stepped into the house. It was dark but warm and smelled of a fire in the fireplace, tobacco and the remains of lunch. Maybe a hearty soup.

"Here, have a seat," Altamont said. "Can I get you anything? Tea?"

"No, thank you."

He had gestured toward a worn cloth recliner and when she sat, she could feel the warmth of the previous body in the cushion. The man she assumed was Charles Altamont sat across from her in a matching, but less worn chair. This one faced the fire and although the wood was down to a few red embers, she could feel its heat.

"Now, why are you asking about Charles Altamont?" he asked.

"I'm looking into the disappearance of this woman," she said. Pauling held up the photo of Noelle Sinclair.

"And what does that have to do with me?"

"That's what I'd like to find out. This

woman, Noelle Sinclair, had as her last known address a building owned by you at that time. I understand you sold the property, but I'm assuming you must know her, or at least, know of her."

"That's a big assumption."

"Not really. Generally, if I own a building and someone is living there, I'm probably going to know about it, unless I have a property management firm who places tenants without my knowledge, which would also be very rare. I'm also guessing by your caginess in refusing to answer my question directly that you do in fact, know her, but are hesitant to tell me anything because you aren't really sure who I am and why I'm asking."

He sat back in his chair as if she had shoved him with both hands.

"I admire your blunt approach," he finally admitted. "So you're not with the police?"

"No. I'm a private investigator."

"And who is your client?"

"I'm not at liberty to say."

"Then I can't help you."

"Why not? Why does it matter who hired me?"

"Because I have no idea who you are and although I have no information for you why would I share it with you if I did?"

Pauling took out her drivers license and a small leather id case with her photo and a copy of her New York private investigators license.

"Here," she said. She handed him the items and he studied them, then handed them back.

"I believe you," he said. "You have that kind of face anyway. But it still doesn't tell me who hired you."

"A law firm hired me. I believe their client is a woman named Josephine Moutier Reacher."

The man's eyes widened almost imperceptibly, but Pauling caught the change.

"I see," he said.

"So, again, do you know where I can find Noelle Sinclair?"

The man glanced over at the fire, as if making a decision. His head swiveled back to face Pauling.

"I don't know where she is, and I wish I did."

"Can you explain?"

The old man dug tobacco out of his pipe, packed it into the bowl and used a match to light it. He puffed and soon a cloud of smoke rose above his head.

"My wife died several years ago," he said. "Her name was Kate. She was a strong woman from a broken family. Her father abandoned the family when she was two and her mother worked two or three jobs at a time during most of my wife's childhood. When my wife was sixteen, her mother died. Kate vowed that her children would always have a home with food on the table and plenty of love to go around."

Pauling had noticed the lack of any signs of family members in the house. There was a portrait of Altamont and his wife in the hall-way, which meant she knew what he was about to say.

"Of course, as fate would have it, we were unable to have children."

"So you adopted."

"Not exactly," he replied. "We were going

to, but then we heard about a young girl in desperate need of help. It appeared that she, too, had an absentee father and a recently deceased mother. We were told she was in danger, so her name was changed and she came to live with us, understanding it was only temporary."

"Why would it have been temporary?"

He sighed. "Because the world is a dangerous place for young women. And we were told it was especially the young woman you're asking about."

"Why, though?"

"We were never told. The opportunity simply came up that we could help protect a young woman with no father or mother and my wife jumped at the chance."

"And then?"

"And then one day, she was gone."

"Gone? As in, she left or was she taken?"

"She was taken by the same person who found us and asked us to care for her."

"And who was this person?"

The old man stared into the fire as he said the name.

"Josephine Moutier Reacher."

Pauling had guessed as much. But one thing was still bothering her.

"You said the girl's Dad abandoned the family. And that the mother was killed when the girl was quite young."

The old man nodded.

"How did the girl's mother die?"

The light in the man's pipe darkened and then went out.

"She was murdered," he said.

15

Ronald Richard Kingsley was in a foul mood. The dinner with his assistant, an ambush, really, couldn't have gone worse. She rebuffed him and despite his veiled threats, walked out on him.

He would carefully terminate her position within his office, or simply transfer her if the threat of a lawsuit became too much to risk.

Now, he was in the back of his armored SUV with his chief of staff, Bertram Pohler, who was in the process of making his day even worse.

"The American made contact with our old friend Altamont," Pohler said.

"Jesus Christ – how did she find him?"

"We're not sure, but she spent the better part of an hour with him, so she may have more information than we want her to have."

"An hour? Good God," Kingsley said. "He could have acted out the entire thing for her in that amount of time."

"True. So we have some decisions to make."

"I thought we made our decision and the Collective is handling it."

"Time may be of the essence here, sir," Pohler continued. "I have no doubt they were able to replace the individual who failed in Marrakesh, but I don't know how long it will take for that person to intercept the American. If she discovers too much before then, it could create additional problems."

"What do you suggest?" Kingsley snapped. "Bring me solutions, not problems."

"I suggest we supply some extra insurance immediately," Pohler said. "We can have a man go after the American tonight and if he fails, well, then the Collective should be attempting shortly thereafter."

"As long as 'our' man is no way connected to us, I have no problem with it," Kingsley said, his voice bored. "Plenty of money in the discretionary fund, correct?"

"Correct."

Kingsley sighed. He was frustrated. So many of the mistakes he'd made continued to reverberate through his life and he wished he could make them stop.

They almost all had to do with young women who refused to cooperate.

He'd been harsh.

Way too harsh, way too often.

He was more measured now, but that didn't matter. The past was like an angry ocean that could cough up a rogue wave now and then just to marvel at its ensuing destruction.

16

The network of law enforcement professionals is as vast as the reach of the law itself. It took multiple emails and phone calls but eventually Pauling was able to connect with a retired homicide inspector from the Paris police department, which went by the fancy name of *Paris Police Prefecture.*

The retired detective was a woman and her name was Dephine. Pauling was able to reach her by phone. Altamont had given Pauling the name of the missing girl's murdered mother.

"Monica Sinclair, you say?" the retired detective asked her.

"Yes."

"I remember her," Dephine said. Her voice was crisp and clear. Pauling figured she hadn't retired that long ago. "Unsolved. Went cold."

"Any suspects?"

"Not really. The victim died of a broken neck. She was found in a park. No witnesses. No fingerprints. No one with a motive. We figured she might have been meeting a man there, or something, but we could never make any progress. Her husband was of absolutely no help, I remember that. He wouldn't talk to us, other than to confirm his alibi."

Pauling was stunned.

"Husband? I thought he had abandoned the family."

"He did, but he was still her husband."

"He wasn't a suspect?"

"No, he had an alibi. He'd been out of town on a job with multiple co-workers who were all able to vouch for his whereabouts."

"Was it possible he hired someone?"

"We looked into that but he didn't have any money and she didn't either. She was a secretary, and he was a part-time laborer getting work when he could."

"What happened to the daughter?" Pauling asked. "Noelle."

"She was placed with a family, if I recall. Why?"

"I'm having some trouble tracking her down."

"Maybe she got back in touch with her father," Dephine said. "I doubt it, because he was a real piece of work and wanted nothing to do with his dead wife and their daughter."

Pauling considered what she'd just been told. There'd been no mention of Jack Reacher's mother and she made a mental note to track down that connection. It would probably explain a lot. But that could come later, for now, she had to attack the strongest leads.

"Do you remember the husband's name?" Pauling asked.

Dephine hesitated. "It started with a G. Let me think. It was kind of a strange name, too...Gabin. That's it. I always thought it was a typo – you know, that it should be Gavin. But it's spelled with a *b*. Gabin. Gabin Sinclair."

Pauling knew better than to ask for a copy of the original homicide file. Not that she thought getting her hands on it would be too difficult. It was an older, cold case. Worst case scenario one of her internet sleuths would be able to find it.

Pauling thanked the detective and hung up, then immediately placed a call to her freelance investigator back in New York. She told him about Gabin Sinclair and asked for an expedited search.

There was enough information –Gabin's name, the murdered mother and Noelle – to make her confident the husband could be found, if he was still alive. Pauling wasn't making any assumptions in this case.

Satisfied, she drove back to her hotel, left the Audi with the valet, and returned to her room.

She was tired and famished.

Pauling ordered grilled fish and a bottle of white wine from room service, showered and changed. In the living space of her room off to one side was a small desk and white leather chair. She'd put her laptop there and now she sat in front of it.

Pauling checked the status of Tallon's flight to Paris. It would be arriving later in the evening and he would take a car to the hotel. She felt a little flutter in her chest at the thought of seeing him again. She missed him. Her body missed his touch, plain and simple.

A notification appeared in her email application and she opened a message from her investigator. He'd already found Gabin Sinclair. He was in Pitie-Salpetriere Hospital. He had cancer and was terminal.

"Damn it," Pauling said. She reads the contents of what her researcher had found.

She was about to send an email when there was a knock on the door.

She went and opened it, her stomach growling at the prospect of a good meal and a man pushed his way in. He was dressed all in black and had a pistol with a silencer in his hand.

Pauling had donned a pair of jeans and a t-shirt. She was barefoot. The man was bigger than her and she quickly realized how precarious her situation was.

Seeing she was clearly unarmed, the man's eyes glanced around the room. He took in the laptop, the suitcase next to the bed, and Pauling's wet hair.

She knew what he was thinking: a woman alone, just out of the shower, unarmed.

He kicked the door shut behind him and Pauling instinctively lashed out. He had not wanted to risk turning around and using his free hand to shut the door, so he had chosen to play it safe: he'd used his left leg and simply kicked backward, leaving all of his weight on his right leg.

That was Pauling's target.

She twisted at the waist and swept her left leg in an arc. It connected with solid impact on the side of the man's knee. It was a perfectly executed kick and she heard the knee give as her foot slammed into it.

The human knee, although a wonder in some ways, was also a very vulnerable joint. Impacts from the side could be especially damaging and Pauling's kick was no exception. The man's leg buckled and he fell sideways with no way to stop his fall as he had been off balance to begin with.

He crashed to the floor, but the gun was

still in his grip. He squeezed the trigger and Pauling heard the spit of the silencer.

Plaster crashed to the floor from the wall behind her.

Pauling wasted no time in choosing her plan of action.

She could wrestle the man for the gun, but he outweighed her and on the ground, the advantage she had over his injured knee would be rendered mute.

Instead, she vaulted over him, threw open the door and ran.

It was the right choice.

The door slammed behind her and there was no way the man was going to catch her. She was certain her kick had torn some ligaments and damaged some cartilage. A footrace was to her advantage.

She bypassed the elevator and went to the stairwell. Her room was only on the third floor.

Pauling raced down the steps, threw open the door to the lobby and raced to the front desk.

"Call the police," she said. "Someone just tried to kill me."

17

Sleep when you can.

During his time on active duty in the military, it was a motto Tallon and his men had lived by.

Sleep when you can. Eat when you can. Even if you aren't tired or hungry.

Tallon had a been a professional sleeper: if there had been a thirty-minute gap of down time, he had always been able to doze off instantly and come awake immediately at the end of the thirty minutes. Without an alarm. Wide awake.

Old habits died hard and since Pauling had booked him a spacious seat on the flight to Paris, he'd had a dreamless snooze as he'd crossed the Atlantic.

Now, they were getting ready to land and he was fully awake.

Despite all of his international travel, he'd never actually been to Paris and was looking forward to it. It was no coincidence the City of Lights had escaped his travel plans; he'd made a living going to active hot spots around the world and although it had certainly been home to some terrorist acts, none of them had resulted in a contract involving Tallon.

For him, it would be a new experience.

It had been two weeks since he'd seen Pauling. They'd spent a great week in New York at her place but he still felt the pull of his ranch. They were in limbo: Pauling still had her loft apartment in Manhattan, and he had his ranch. They both felt comfortable at each other's homes, but neither one had made the move to sell their place and move in with the other.

For now, it was working.

But he wasn't sure if it was a good, long-term solution. And if Pauling really, deep down, *wanted* a long-term solution.

Neither one of them was getting any younger.

Maybe they were too set in their ways.

The plane touched down and the light in the cabin came on. Tallon had only packed a small bag so it shouldn't take him too long to get through Customs and join Pauling.

Eventually, the passengers began to disembark and Tallon got off the plane.

He didn't see her, but minutes after he stepped off the aircraft, the passenger from ten rows behind him exited the plane, too.

She was tall, athletic, and had skin the color of dark chocolate.

Star.

18

W hen the police interview was done – it was sort of an inter- rogation but Pauling felt like the French police preferred the gentler term – the first person she saw was Michael Tallon.

"Here I thought we were going on vacation," he said as they embraced. The police had already searched the hotel and had not found the man who broke into Pauling's room. The hotel had security cameras, but the footage revealed no new clues.

"How are you doing?" Tallon asked. He'd taken a cab straight from the airport to Pauling's hotel and had been more than a little surprised at the scene he walked into.

"Well, considering that I answered the door blindly because I thought it was my room service dinner...I'm starving," she answered.

They dropped Tallon's bag in Pauling's new room – the hotel had upgraded her to a suite – and went out for dinner. They found a quiet restaurant and had a hearty meal. Pauling used the time to fill Tallon in on everything that had happened thus far.

After a dessert of coffee and ice cream, they returned to the room.

There, they made love and fell promptly asleep.

In the morning, their passion called for another round. Afterward, they planned.

"So this Gabin guy – do you really think he'll be able to tell us anything?" Tallon asked. "The guy ditched his wife and kid way back when. He probably has no clue where she is or what she even looks like."

"True," Pauling admitted. "But right now, it's the only lead I have."

"Where's some of this Parisian coffee I've

heard so much about?" Tallon asked with a smile. He ordered a pot from room service and soon he was pouring them both a big cup of rich black coffee.

Once fully caffeinated, they retrieved the Audi and drove to Pitie-Salpetriere Hospital. Pauling was worried: they weren't family and they didn't know why Gabin was in the hospital. How would they be allowed to see him?

In the end, they simply explained they wished to see him as they were friends of the family. The nurses initially seemed skeptical but once they checked the computer, their attitudes changed.

Pauling knew why; Gabin was terminal. And at this point, they weren't about to refuse anyone who wanted to say goodbye.

They were led to the seventh floor, which turned out to be the cancer ward. Gabin was located on the east end which they soon learned was reserved for those with a terminal prognosis of less than three months.

The man was skeletal, devoid of hair, with bloodshot gray eyes. Every vein in his exposed flesh was visible.

To Pauling, the room smelled of antiseptic, death and decay.

"Mr. Sinclair?" she asked.

He looked at her, opened his mouth to speak. It took him nearly ten seconds to utter the words. "Qui etes vous?" *Who are you?*

Pauling knew enough French to answer. She explained they were looking into the murder of his wife.

His face remained impassive. Pained, most likely, but Pauling assumed that was the cancer. There was a television in the corner of the room tuned to local television. Gabin watched it. Pauling thought he wasn't going to answer.

Finally, he did.

"She died like the whore she was," he said in French. Pauling translated for Tallon.

"Why do you say that?" she asked.

The man's face had turned red. His breath came in shorter gasps but the anger seemed to make him stronger.

"Why should I tell you? I never told the cops a thing."

Pauling remembered that's what Dephine had told her. "Maybe so we can catch her killer. The cops still don't know who murdered her."

"He did me a favor," Gabin said. His death mask now bore a slight grin. Dephine was right; this man didn't want to help and was a real piece of work.

"Tell him his daughter needs help," Tallon suggested.

Pauling thought it was a good idea – the man clearly had hated his wife and apparently still did. Maybe he would tell them what he knew for his daughter's sake. She asked him the question.

"Daughter? I don't have a daughter," he replied with a sneer. His teeth were gray and filmy.

Pauling knew what he meant by that – he said his wife was a whore, which meant he probably had questioned if the baby was his.

"Noelle Sinclair isn't your daughter?" Pauling asked.

"That girl bastard?" Gabin made a sound with his mouth. Somewhere behind a scoff and a cough. "Not mine."

"Whose was she then?"

Gabin was watching the television. He

started to cackle with laughter. Drool ran out the side of his mouth and dribbled down his chin.

He raised a shaking hand at the television. One veiny, pale finger pointed at the screen.

"His," he said.

19

Getting a gun was easy. They still had rentable lockers at the airport and Gunnella Bohm and the Zurich Collective had thought of everything.

A man dressed as a limousine driver had slipped Star a key. She had gone to the locker and retrieved the leather briefcase and then booked a rental car.

Inside the car, she opened the briefcase.

A lovely little Walther PPK, .38 caliber with a silencer. A nod to James Bond, she thought.

At an intersection, she tossed the brief-case from the car. There was nothing else inside – all of the documents had been sent to her phone, encrypted of course. She'd already gone over them and deleted their contents.

She knew her target was a woman named Lauren Pauling.

Star hadn't killed a lot of women – most of her targets were men. But she had no qualms about ending the life of someone with whom she shared a gender.

It was money in the bank, whether the blood she let contained higher concentrations of estrogen or testosterone was beside the point.

Paris wasn't new to her, she'd visited the city both for work and pleasure. Getting to the hospital was no problem. A spotter had relayed the location of Pauling and said she was still inside the facility.

Star parked her rental car, slipped the weapon inside her three-quarter length jacket and took up a position at the café next to the hospital. She supposed it was favored by people visiting their loved ones in the hospital – when they needed a break from what was probably a distressing situation they could pop over to the café for nourishment and to regain the energy required to stay relentlessly upbeat.

Star had watched her grandmother, her only living relative as far as she knew, die in a horrible hospital in south central Los Angeles. It had been a horrible, unnerving, soul-crushing experience. One she worked very hard to erase from her memory. But it always lingered there and now, as she watched the hospital's front entrance, she felt a momentary thudding sensation in the pit of her stomach. Her grandmother had died a horrible death, and Star felt that every time she killed someone, it was another small payback for what the world had done to the only person she had ever loved.

The sky had thankfully cleared up and there was no threat of rain. This was good for Star because she had noted several women wearing scarves or hiding under umbrellas, making it very difficult to ID her target. But now, the sun was out, and it seemed the Parisians were basking in the sunlight.

By the time she finished her third cup of coffee she felt the caffeine kick in and she asked for a bottled water. It would do her no good to have an unsteady hand. She'd been at the café for nearly two hours and although she knew Paris was famous for people enjoying four-hour dinners, she felt she might be making herself too noticeable and was thinking about changing locations.

And then Lauren Pauling stepped out of the front door of the hospital.

20

As he pushed through the front door of the hospital and walked outside, Michael Tallon was momentarily surprised by the bright sunlight. When they'd arrived less than an hour ago, it had been gray and gloomy.

Now it was like was a warm summer day.

"Glad the sun came out," Pauling said. "That was depressing in there."

"He may have cancer, but that man is dying of bitterness," Tallon observed. "I think it ate him up his whole life and the illness just came in to finish him off."

"At least we know–" Pauling started to say, but Tallon didn't hear her.

Something had taken his attention. It was the black woman. She was walking toward them and he recognized her. But from where?

And then he remembered.

The plane.

She'd been on his flight.

Paris had more than its fair share of African Americans, so it wasn't a surprise to see her. It was just a coincidence.

But Tallon hated coincidences and had been taught at many times in his life to ignore them at his own peril.

So he reacted by stepping up next to Pauling and putting his hand on her shoulder.

When he saw the black woman shift her body as well, he knew what was about to happen.

He pushed Pauling and sent her sprawling to the ground at the same time he lunged forward.

The woman's hand slid from her overcoat and Tallon saw the gun – a small caliber automatic with a silencer and it tracked Pauling as she fell.

He flung himself at the woman and managed to hit her arm just as the gun coughed and spat a bullet.

The woman looked at him, surprise and anger in her eyes.

She let go of the gun and elbowed Tallon in the nose.

It surprised him. He hadn't expected she would let go of the gun. The blow shocked him with pain and his eyes watered but it wasn't enough to knock him unconscious.

He felt blood gush down into his mouth and his hands grasped the woman's wrist. He heard the gun clatter and then she was out from beneath him.

As he struggled to get to his feet, he felt a pain in his ribs and knew she'd kicked him hard. His breath wooshed from his lungs and he staggered. She kicked him again but this time he caught her shin and lunged upward. The woman landed on her back, but rolled and bounced right up.

A knife was in her hand.

It was long and thin – a spring-loaded stiletto – and she was already thrusting it at him when her body recoiled. She stared at

Tallon, uncomprehending. A hole appeared just above her left eye. Tallon heard the gun behind him cough again and the bullet staggered the black woman again. It knocked her head backward and she momentarily stopped, swayed and then fell to the ground.

Tallon turned.

Pauling had the gun with the silencer attached, smoke curling from the barrel.

"Thanks," he said to her. "I was getting my ass kicked."

21

This time, Pauling was brought to Paris Police Prefecture, headquarters for the city's police force. It was an impressive structure located at 1 Rue de Latece with loads of security out front.

Unlike the attack at the hotel, this was a homicide that had taken place in broad daylight. There had been swarms of policemen on the scene and now, Pauling and Tallon were whisked through the front entrance of the building and taken to separate interrogation rooms.

Thankfully, the retired homicide detective, Dephine, was contacted to corroborate

Pauling's version of events. The Parisian authorities also verified Pauling's history with the FBI and the rest of her information. However, that didn't make them any less skeptical of the supposed sequence of events.

"So you're telling me he just coughed up this information after years of silence?" the lead detective asked. His name was Riegels and he was head of the cold case unit. He was a fireplug of a man with thinning blonde hair and a red face. He was nearly as wide as he was tall. "And that he identified the man supposedly having an affair with his wife by pointing him out on the television?"

"Yes," Pauling replied. "But he told us his wife did, in fact, work as a secretary for Kingsley. He claims the two had an affair and she was probably killed because she had become pregnant with Kingsley's child. I know it sounds preposterous," Pauling continued. "But why don't you ask him yourself?"

"I would, but he's dead," Riegels said. "The hospital said he went into cardiac arrest about ten minutes after you left. How convenient."

Pauling kept her cool. She would contact an attorney if she had to, but she preferred to work this out on her own.

"Look, it shouldn't be that difficult to investigate," she said. "Did Monica Sinclair work in the office of Ronald Kingsley? There should be employment records somewhere, probably in the original case file. It must say for whom she was working. If so, talk to Kingsley. Even better, find the girl and do a DNA test to see if Kingsley is her biological father, like Gabin Sinclair claimed."

"And if all that is true, then what?" Riegels asked. "Charge Kingsley with murder without any real evidence? For Christ's sake – the man's a legend. He lunches regularly with the Queen!"

Pauling fought to keep her patience. "Look, I'm not going to tell you how to do your job. But as far as I know, this is new information on one of your cold cases. Why don't you at least start talking to some people and see where it takes you?"

Riegels clearly didn't like being told how to do his job, but he changed the subject.

"I'd like you to stop working on this case until further notice."

Pauling raised an eyebrow. "Are you sure you have the authority to tell me that?"

"Maybe yes, maybe no."

She decided to cut her losses. "Fine. I'm going back to my hotel and looking for flights out of here anyway. Paris is too exciting for me."

Now it was Riegels' turn to express skepticism. "Believe me, we'll be keeping tabs on you and your friend."

"Don't make me get my lawyer in here," Pauling said.

That was enough to make the detective drop his line of thinking.

"We'll be in touch," he said.

She was shown out and soon joined Tallon outside. They took a cab back to the hotel and asked the concierge to retrieve the Audi that was still at the hospital.

"Now what?" Tallon asked as he opened the door to Pauling's room.

A woman stood there. She was young, blonde and quite pretty.

"Now we take down Kingsley once and for all," the young woman said.

Pauling stepped around Tallon and studied their surprise visitor.

"Hello Noelle," she said.

22

Kingsley was irate. His right-hand man, Pohler, was late. And of all things to be late for, this was not it.

He stood in the middle of his home in the most trendy part of Paris. It was a glorious mansion with seven bedrooms eight bathrooms and a garden that was photographed annually by various clubs and societies dedicated to that sort of thing.

The garden was a place of great peace, but Kingsley wasn't having any of it. He was beside himself. The news that the assassin sent by Bohm had botched the job before his man even had a chance was a disaster. The failed attempt had no doubt put the American investigator on notice and she would not be caught unawares again.

That left Kingsley with what?

Shit, is what he thought. *That's what I'm left with.*

The door finally opened and Kingsley turned. "Goddamnit Pohler–"

His words caught in his throat.

Gunnella Bohm stood in the doorway.

"Jesus, you're enormous," was all Kingsley could say. He'd never met her in person, but he'd heard all of the stories about her. He'd always thought they were exaggeration, but now he realized they really hadn't done her justice. It was like someone had crossed a Viking conqueror with an Amazonian queen.

Bohm stepped aside and two men carried in the body of Bertram Pohler. They tossed it on the carpet. Kingsley felt a momentary twinge for his second-in-command. He had not treated the man well over the course of time and now he was dead. Shot in the head, apparently.

A second body was tossed to the ground, as well. Kingsley didn't recognize the man, but knew it was the "insurance" Pohler had hired but was taken out before he'd had a chance to fulfill the contract.

"Any more bodies?" Kingsley quipped.

"You never should have taken matters into your own hands," Bohm said. "A clear violation of our operating agreement."

"Give me a break," Kingsley said, his voice weak. "You had two chances and you blew it. Now you're lecturing me?"

"No, I'm not here to lecture you," she said.

Kingsley recognized the threat. "Don't even think about," he said.

The man next to Bohm lifted his hand. An oversized automatic with an enormous silencer was attached.

"Go to hell," Kingsley said.

The gun fired and Kingsley jolted twice. Two shots. Spaced within an inch apart over his heart.

He dropped to the floor.

Bohm looked around.

"Burn this dump to the ground," she said.

23

P auling studied the woman's face. There was no doubt.

It was Noelle Sinclair.

"Why don't you start at the beginning?" Pauling said.

"Josephine Reacher was a kind woman who helped a lot of people, including my Mom," Noelle explained. "After my mother was killed, Mrs. Reacher sent me to live with the Altamonts. But word got back that my mother's death was more complicated than it first appeared and I might be in danger, too. So I was sent to Morocco and that's where I've been living."

"Until..."

"Until someone tried to kill me and I knew that I could never rest." She smiled, a bit of mischief in her eyes. "That's why I hired you."

Pauling shook her head. "*You* hired me? I should have known."

"I did my research and knew you had a connection to the Reachers," she said. "And that you'd been an FBI agent." She glanced at Tallon. "I did my research on you, too, and learned the two of you have handled some intense cases so I figured you would be the perfect team to help me put an end to this nightmare once and for all."

"Thanks for the compliment," he said.

"I needed someone to investigate on my behalf but I couldn't just hire you. I would have had to tell you my story and I highly doubt you would have believed it. Plus, I couldn't give you cold, hard proof. So I pretended that Mrs. Reacher's will required it. It was the only way I could figure out how to get you involved." There were the beginnings of tears in her eyes. "I'm sorry I tricked you."

"But didn't all of that take money?"

Pauling asked. "My flight, the hotel, the two million dollar paycheck I'm supposed to get?"

"My stepdad gave me a chunk of money when my stepmom died. And, hopefully once we expose Kingsley, I'll take a DNA test. As far as I know, I'm his only offspring."

"And he's a very wealthy man," Pauling said.

"Aren't we getting ahead of ourselves? How are we planning on taking down Kingsley, if in fact we can prove he killed your mother and tried to kill you?"

"I don't have a plan other than what we're doing right now," Noelle said. "I just needed someone to break open the case. I read on the news about the shooting at the hospital, and I know that creep who used to be living with my Mom is there, dying of cancer."

"He actually died right after we talked to him."

"Good," Noelle said. "I put two and two together so I came here. To thank you. And to apologize for getting you involved."

"I still don't understand," Pauling said. "If you knew about Kingsley–"

"I didn't, not for sure. And Gabin

wouldn't talk to me. He refused to even see me."

"How did you know about our conversation?"

"A small bribe to a friend of a friend and a listening device was placed in his room, just in case."

She held up her phone. "Connected wirelessly, it was like I was right there with you."

"So that's it, then?" Pauling asked. "We're done? We're going to let the Parisian authorities investigate the case?"

"Yes and no," Noelle said. "Kingsley is going down, if he hasn't done so already. But I need to know who's helping him. Someone arranged to have that killer in Marrakesh. I want to make sure there are no more open contracts on me."

"I can help you with that," Tallon said.

Pauling and Noelle both looked at him.

"The woman who tried to kill us at the hospital?" he said. "Her name was Star. I've heard of her."

"From where?"

Tallon sighed. "It's a little hard to believe but I keep in touch with some guys I've worked with in and out of the military. Some of them are lone mercenaries, usually taking elimination contracts."

"They're assassins?"

Tallon nodded. "They all work in this loosely based organization called The Department of Murder."

"Are you serious?" Noelle asked.

"I'm afraid so," Tallon replied. "It's a fluid group, but occasionally, contacts are made. After we were nearly killed, I made some calls. And I was able to trace Star's contract back to a woman I know. I'm sure she was the same person who hired the killer in Marrakesh."

"Who is she?"

"Her name is Gunnella Bohm. People thought she was killed long ago, but turns out, she's alive and well."

There was a pause.

"For now," he added.

TWO MONTHS LATER

ZURICH, SWITZERLAND

"MORE."

Gunnella Bohm was on her back. Her hands and feet were tied and she was still recovering from an earth-shaking orgasm.

Her latest prostitute was a sadist and for once, Bohm had allowed herself to be vulnerable. She was covered in dried wax and burn marks covered vast swaths of her pale flesh.

The ropes used to secure the big woman to her own bed, in her multi-million dollar penthouse apartment, weren't for show. They were real knots, and despite Bohm's super-human strength, were holding her fast.

The woman, a professional dominatrix named Vixen, had left the room to get more champagne.

She'd been gone for nearly fifteen minutes.

"You are beginning to anger me. You will suffer–" Bohm began to say, but she stopped.

A man had stepped into the room.

He was broad shouldered. Dressed in jeans, a black jacket and a baseball cap. Bohm recognized him.

"Michael Tallon?" she asked. Her voice was normal. If she had any discomfort at being buck naked with her legs spread wide in front of him, she didn't show it.

"Hello Gunnella," he said. "Do you greet all of your guests like this?"

"No, just you," she answered. "You're special. What are you doing here?"

"Something I should have done a long time ago," he said.

Bohm was neither scared nor delusional. Tallon had made no effort to hide his face. She knew what that meant.

"I can make you one of the richest men on Earth," she said. "Whatever they're paying you, I'll triple it."

"No one's paying me anything," he said. "This is a courtesy on behalf of the young woman you tried to kill in Morocco, and all of the other innocent people you've done away with."

"Whatever they're paying you, I'll multiply it by ten."

"Zero times ten is zero."

Bohm glanced over Tallon's shoulder.

"She's okay," he said. "You two make a cute couple."

Her eyes flared. "What is this?" she snapped at him.

He raised his pistol and shot her twice in the head.

"It's the end of the story," Tallon replied.

BUY THE NEXT BOOK IN THE SERIES!

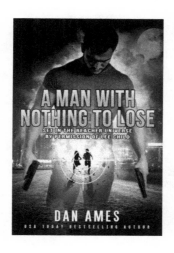

CLICK HERE TO BUY

A USA TODAY BESTSELLING BOOK

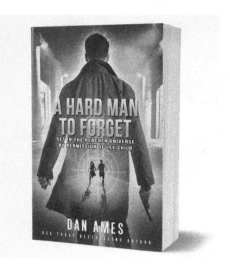

Book One in The JACK REACHER Cases

CLICK HERE TO BUY NOW

ABOUT THE AUTHOR

Dan Ames is a USA TODAY Bestselling Author, Amazon Kindle #1 bestseller, Good-Reads Readers Choice finalist and winner of the Independent Book Award for Crime Fiction.

www.authordanames.com
dan@authordanames.com

ALSO BY DAN AMES

THE JACK REACHER CASES

The JACK REACHER Cases #1 (A Hard Man To Forget)

The JACK REACHER Cases #2 (The Right Man For Revenge)

The JACK REACHER Cases #3 (A Man Made For Killing)

The JACK REACHER Cases #4 (The Last Man To Murder)

The JACK REACHER Cases #5 (The Man With No Mercy)

The JACK REACHER Cases #6 (A Man Out For Blood)

The JACK REACHER Cases #7 (A Man Beyond The Law)

The JACK REACHER Cases #8 (The Man Who Walks Away)

The JACK REACHER Cases (The Man Who Strikes Fear)

The JACK REACHER Cases (The Man Who

Stands Tall)

The JACK REACHER Cases (The Man Who
Works Alone)

The Jack Reacher Cases (A Man Built For Justice)

The JACK REACHER Cases #13 (A Man Born for
Battle)

The JACK REACHER Cases #14 (The Perfect
Man for Payback)

The JACK REACHER Cases #15 (The Man
Whose Aim Is True)

The JACK REACHER Cases #16 (The Man Who
Dies Here)

The JACK REACHER Cases #17 (The Man With
Nothing To Lose)

The JACK REACHER Cases #18 (The Man Who
Never Goes Back)

The JACK REACHER Cases #19 (The Man From
The Shadows)

The JACK REACHER CASES #20 (The Man
Behind The Gun)

JACK REACHER'S SPECIAL INVESTIGATORS

BOOK ONE: DEAD MEN WALKING

BOOK TWO: GAME OVER

BOOK THREE: LIGHTS OUT

BOOK FOUR: NEVER FORGIVE, NEVER
FORGET

BOOK FIVE: HIT THEM FAST, HIT
THEM HARD

BOOK SIX: FINISH THE FIGHT

THE JOHN ROCKNE MYSTERIES

DEAD WOOD (John Rockne Mystery #1)

HARD ROCK (John Rockne Mystery #2)

COLD JADE (John Rockne Mystery #3)

LONG SHOT (John Rockne Mystery #4)

EASY PREY (John Rockne Mystery #5)

BODY BLOW (John Rockne Mystery #6)

THE WADE CARVER THRILLERS

MOLLY (Wade Carver Thriller #1)

SUGAR (Wade Carver Thriller #2)

ANGEL (Wade Carver Thriller #3)

THE WALLACE MACK THRILLERS

THE KILLING LEAGUE (Wallace Mack Thriller #1)

THE MURDER STORE (Wallace Mack Thriller #2)

FINDERS KILLERS (Wallace Mack Thriller #3)

THE MARY COOPER MYSTERIES

DEATH BY SARCASM (Mary Cooper
Mystery #1)

MURDER WITH SARCASTIC INTENT (Mary
Cooper Mystery #2)

GROSS SARCASTIC HOMICIDE (Mary Cooper
Mystery #3)

THE CIRCUIT RIDER (WESTERNS)

THE CIRCUIT RIDER (Circuit Rider #1)

KILLER'S DRAW (Circuit Rider #2)

THE RAY MITCHELL THRILLERS

THE RECRUITER

KILLING THE RAT

HEAD SHOT

STANDALONE THRILLERS:

KILLER GROOVE (Rockne & Cooper Mystery #1)

BEER MONEY (Burr Ashland Mystery #1)

TO FIND A MOUNTAIN (A WWII Thriller)

BOX SETS:

AMES TO KILL

GROSSE POINTE PULP

GROSSE POINTE PULP 2

TOTAL SARCASM

WALLACE MACK THRILLER COLLECTION

SHORT STORIES:

THE GARBAGE COLLECTOR

BULLET RIVER

SCHOOL GIRL

HANGING CURVE

SCALE OF JUSTICE

FREE BOOKS AND MORE

Would you like a FREE copy
of my story BULLET RIVER and the chance
to win a free Kindle?

Then sign up for the DAN AMES BOOK
CLUB:

For special offers and new releases, sign
up here

Printed in the USA
CPSIA information can be obtained
at www.ICGtesting.com
LVHW040958140724
785261LV00030B/91

9 798700 650397